The Complete
Cloudy With a Chance
of Meatballs

Cloudy With a Chance of Meatballs
Pickles to Pittsburgh

Written by Judi Barrett and drawn by Ron Barrett

Atheneum Books for Young Readers
New York London Toronto Sydney

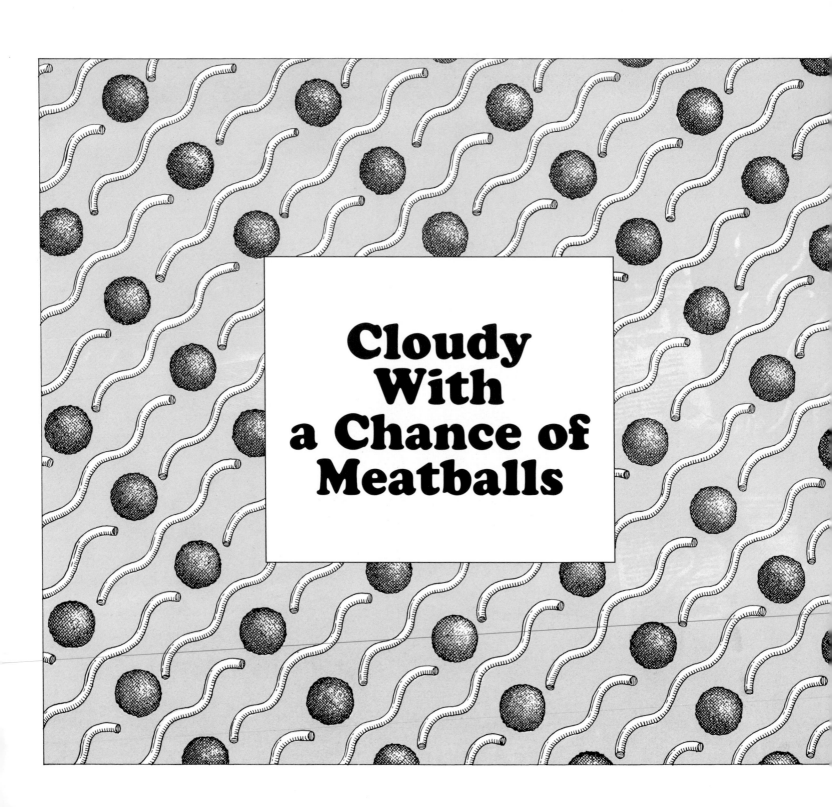

Cloudy
With
a Chance of
Meatballs

We were all sitting around the big kitchen table. It was Saturday morning. Pancake morning. Mom was squeezing oranges for juice. Henry and I were betting on how many pancakes we each could eat. And Grandpa was doing the flipping.

Seconds later, something flew through the air headed toward the kitchen ceiling . . .

. . . and landed right on Henry.

After we realized that the flying object was only a pancake, we all laughed, even Grandpa. Breakfast continued quite uneventfully. All the other pancakes landed in the pan. And all of them were eaten, even the one that landed on Henry.

That night, touched off by the pancake incident at breakfast, Grandpa told us the best tall-tale bedtime story he'd ever told.

"Across an ocean, over lots of huge bumpy mountains, across three hot deserts, and one smaller ocean . . .

. . . there lay the tiny town of Chewandswallow.

In most ways, it was very much like any other tiny town. It had a Main Street lined with stores, houses with trees and gardens around them, a schoolhouse, about three hundred people, and some assorted cats and dogs.

But there were no food stores in the town of Chewandswallow. They didn't need any. The sky supplied all the food they could possibly want.

The only thing that was really different about Chewandswallow was its weather. It came three times a day, at breakfast, lunch, and dinner. Everything that everyone ate came from the sky.

Whatever the weather served, that was what they ate.

But it never rained rain. It never snowed snow. And it never blew just wind. It rained things like soup and juice. It snowed mashed potatoes and green peas. And sometimes the wind blew in storms of hamburgers.

The people could watch the weather report on television in the morning and they would even hear a prediction for the next day's food.

When the townspeople went outside, they carried their plates, cups, glasses, forks, spoons, knives and napkins with them. That way they would always be prepared for any kind of weather.

If there were leftovers, and there usually were, the people took them home and put them in their refrigerators in case they got hungry between meals.

The menu varied.

By the time they woke up in the morning, breakfast was coming down.

After a brief shower of orange juice, low clouds of sunny-side up eggs moved in followed by pieces of toast. Butter and jelly sprinkled down for the toast. And most of the time it rained milk afterwards.

For lunch one day, frankfurters, already in their rolls, blew in from the northwest at about five miles an hour.

There were mustard clouds nearby. Then the wind shifted to the east and brought in baked beans.

A drizzle of soda finished off the meal.

Dinner one night consisted of lamb chops, becoming heavy at times, with occasional ketchup. Periods of peas and baked potatoes were followed by gradual clearing, with a wonderful Jell-O setting in the west.

The Sanitation Department of Chewandswallow had a rather unusual job for a sanitation department. It had to remove the food that fell on the houses and sidewalks and lawns. The workers cleaned things up after every meal and fed all the dogs and cats. Then they emptied some of it into the surrounding oceans for the fish and turtles and whales to eat. The rest of the food was put back into the earth so that the soil would be richer for the people's flower gardens.

THE SANITATION DEPARTMENT OF CHEWANDSWALLOW

One day there was nothing but Gorgonzola cheese all day long.

The next day there was only broccoli, all overcooked.

And the next day there were brussel sprouts and peanut butter with mayonnaise.

Another day there was a pea soup fog. No one could see where they were going and they could barely find the rest of the meal that got stuck in the fog.

The food was getting larger and larger, and so were the portions. The people were getting frightened. Violent storms blew up frequently. Awful things were happening.

One Tuesday there was a hurricane of bread and rolls all day long and into the night. There were soft rolls and hard rolls, some with seeds and some without. There was white bread and rye and whole wheat toast. Most of it was larger than they had ever seen bread and rolls before. It was a terrible day. Everyone had to stay indoors. Roofs were damaged, and the Sanitation Department was beside itself. The mess took the workers four days to clean up, and the sea was full of floating rolls.

To help out, the people piled up as much bread as they could in their backyards. The birds picked at it a bit, but it just stayed there and got staler and staler.

There was a storm of pancakes one morning and a downpour of maple syrup that nearly flooded the town. A huge pancake covered the school. No one could get it off because of its weight, so they had to close the school.

Lunch one day brought fifteen-inch drifts of cream cheese and jelly sandwiches. Everyone ate themselves sick and the day ended with a stomachache.

There was an awful salt and pepper wind accompanied by an even worse tomato tornado. People were sneezing themselves silly and running to avoid the tomatoes. The town was a mess. There were seeds and pulp everywhere.

The Sanitation Department gave up. The job was too big.

Everyone feared for their lives. They couldn't go outside most of the time. Many houses had been badly damaged by giant meatballs, stores were boarded up and there was no more school for the children.

So a decision was made to abandon the town of Chewand-swallow.

It was a matter of survival.

The people glued together the giant pieces of stale bread sandwich-style with peanut butter . . .

. . . took the absolute necessities with them, and set sail on their rafts for a new land.

After being afloat for a week, they finally reached a small coastal town, which welcomed them. The bread had held up surprisingly well, well enough for them to build temporary houses for themselves out of it.

The children began school again, and the adults all tried to find places for themselves in the new land. The biggest change they had to make was getting used to buying food at a supermarket. They found it odd that the food was kept on shelves, packaged in boxes, cans and bottles. Meat that had to be cooked was kept in large refrigerators. Nothing came down from the sky except rain and snow. The clouds above their heads were not made of fried eggs. No one ever got hit by a hamburger again.

And nobody dared to go back to Chewandswallow to find out what had happened to it. They were too afraid."

Henry and I were awake until the very end of Grandpa's story. I remember his good-night kiss.

The next morning we woke up to see snow falling outside our window.

We ran downstairs for breakfast and ate it a little faster than usual so we could go sleddin with Grandpa.

It's funny, but even as we were sliding down the hill we thought we saw a giant pat of butter at the top, and we could almost smell mashed potatoes.

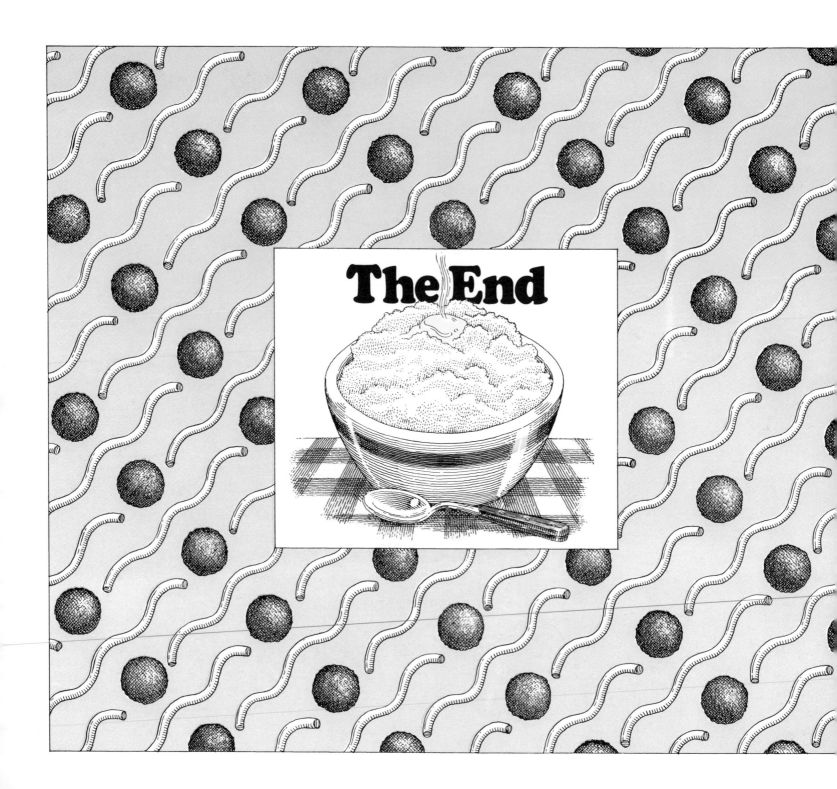

The End

Pickles to Pittsburgh

THE SEQUEL TO

Cloudy With a Chance of Meatballs

Dear Henry and Kate—

I'm having the best vacation ever, but I don't get much rest! I really wish you were here! Our group travels around in a big blue bus and somehow it manages to climb up and down the tallest and bumpiest mountains and around some of the biggest plants I've ever seen.

We've visited many unusual places, met the local people and even helped them out with some of their chores. I'm taking lots of pictures because this place is hard to believe!

Can't wait till I see you next Thursday.

LOVE & HUGS,
GRANDPA

We all missed Grandpa an awful lot . . . his Saturday morning pancakes, his mostly funny jokes, and especially his wonderful bedtime stories. Tomorrow would be Thursday and he'd be home. We could hardly wait to hear where he had been and what he had done.

To pass the time we helped Mom make spaghetti and meatballs for dinner. Henry made the largest meatballs we'd ever seen. They barely fit into the pot! Mom thanked us for helping but asked that the meatballs be MUCH smaller next time.

After we finished eating, Henry and I cleared the table so we could help bake a special "Welcome Home" cake for Grandpa. It was chocolate with strawberry icing and made in the shape of Grandpa's face. We licked as much of the batter off the spoons as we possibly could.

I took Grandpa's postcard up to my room and put it on the little table beside my bed. I kept staring at it and wondering. The lamplight made bright a photograph of a wonderful place that seemed somehow familiar. I said "Good night" to it and drifted off into my dreams . . .

. . . Surrounded by milky blue skies and with Henry as my co-pilot, we carefully steer our plane through large puffs of mist. Soon we find ourselves soaring over an island, a very lumpy island. From the air it looks like a gigantic feast. Immense vegetables, salads, and desserts lie beneath us. The mountains look like huge loaves of bread.

We decide to take a closer look and prepare ourselves for a bumpy landing. Avoiding some broccoli and narrowly missing a tremendous hamburger on an oversized bun, we come down and taxi on what appear to be giant strips of crisp bacon.

Henry and I step down from the plane and look around in awe. Before us lies a strange but wonderful landscape. We are surrounded by larger-than-life vegetables. Nearby is a lake that smells like breakfast, bordered by leafy jungles of lettuce that resemble a tossed salad.

We try to keep our balance as we walk around the top of a gigantic bagel and past a forest of towering carrots. One is pierced by a tunnel large enough for a car to drive through!

Off in the distance we see popcorn snowing down onto the peaks of enormous rolls. Way above our heads, high up in trees that look like broccoli, chubby birds are nesting in huge shredded wheat biscuits.

Ahead of us, at the end of a long road, lies what looks like an abandoned town. Eager to know where we are, we start walking toward it.

Sweet-smelling rain begins to fall. It collects in hundreds of open containers that are lined up in a field beside the road. Lots of orange puddles are everywhere . . . orange juice!

All of a sudden we find ourselves standing in the shadow of a giant tuna fish sandwich being delicately airlifted by helicopter. In the distance another helicopter races off with a jumbo pickle in tow.

When we reach what is left of the town, we see the remnants of a sign welcoming us to a place called Chewandswallow. Somehow, I know I've heard that name somewhere before!

We walk through the entire town in amazement.

Up ahead, lots of workers wearing helmets and dressed in matching uniforms are loading huge potatoes onto a truck.

Other trucks sag under the weight of immense artichokes, enormous eggplants, and massive peas and carrots. Foot-long veal cutlets are stacked up to be packed for shipping.

To the east, the weather is changing and we can see sandwiches raining down. As soon as they land they are piled up neatly, ready for shipment on a freighter anchored down by the shore.

Large reservoirs of milk and cream flow into extra-large containers which are lined up ready to be loaded onto a ship. Printed on the sides of the trucks are the words FALLING FOOD COMPANY—LARGE FOOD FOR LARGE AND SMALL COUNTRIES, FREE.

One of the workers tells us that Chewandswallow used to be a very ordinary little town, except that instead of weather, food rained down from the sky for breakfast, lunch, and dinner.

"Back then," he says, "by some quirk of nature, the falling food grew larger and larger. Storms of gigantic food threatened normal life. So the people took their belongings and sailed away to a new land on rafts made of huge slices of stale bread.

"They returned years later to see what had happened to Chewandswallow. They discovered an endless food supply and decided to create the FALLING FOOD COMPANY."

Now, daily shipments are made to all parts of the world, from the smallest towns to the largest cities. As soon as the food lands it is wrapped, boxed, bottled or packaged, and sent out to people who need it.

. . . throughout the world . . .

Henry and I think this is a great idea. We wish we could stay and work here but I don't think they hire kids!

It's getting late and we hate to leave but we really have to be heading home. Mom's expecting us for dinner. The workers give us a two-foot-wide chocolate chip cookie which we carry back to the plane. It just barely fits through the door!

We buckle up. I rev the engine and we start rolling down the bacon runway. As everyone waves good-bye we can see dinner approaching from the west. Spaghetti and meatballs I think! As we gain altitude, Chewandswallow slowly vanishes into the distance.

My alarm clock woke me with a jolt. It was finally Thursday and I wanted to get to school fast. The sooner I got there the sooner I'd get home and the sooner I'd see Grandpa!

When we got home, we ran as fast as we could into Grandpa's waiting arms. "I brought back something for you," said Grandpa and he gave each of us a very large box containing a chocolate chip cookie he had gotten on his trip. They were the biggest we had ever seen. Almost two feet wide!

Mom made Grandpa's favorite dinner, chicken and dumplings, and we surprised him with our special "Welcome Home" cak He chose the slice with the mustache.

By the time dinner was done it was late and Grandpa was tired. When he was all tucked in bed, we knocked on his door to give him an extra good-night kiss.

Then I told Grandpa the most wonderful, tall-tale bedtime story he'd ever heard. It began, "Surrounded by milky blue skies and with Henry as my co-pilot . . ."

Grandpa stayed awake till the very end. Then he looked at us with a very funny glint in his eye and said, "Wait till I show you the pictures I took on my trip!" And then he drifted off into his own wonderful dreams.

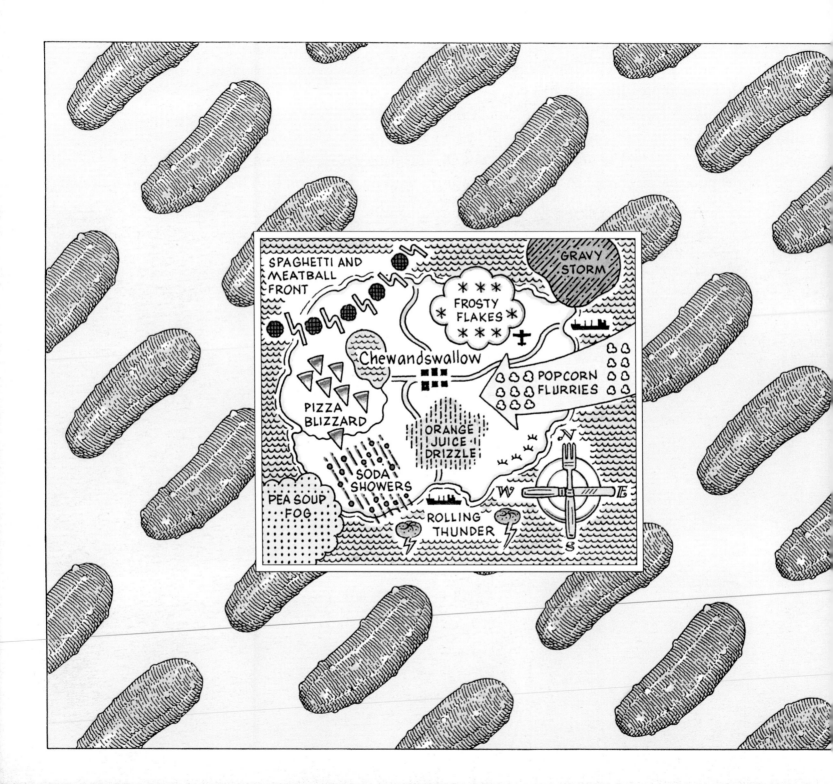

ATHENEUM BOOKS FOR YOUNG READERS • An imprint of Simon & Schuster Children's Publishing Division • 1230 Avenue of the Americas, New York, New York 10020 • *Cloudy With a Chance of Meatballs* text copyright © 1978 by Judi Barrett • *Cloudy With a Chance of Meatballs* illustrations copyright © 1978 by Ron Barrett • *Pickles to Pittsburgh* text copyright © 1997 by Judi Barrett • *Pickles to Pittsburgh* illustrations copyright © 1997 by Judi Barrett and Ron Barrett • All rights reserved, including the right of reproduction in whole or in part in any form. • Atheneum Books for Young Readers is a registered trademark of Simon & Schuster, Inc. • For information about special discounts for bulk purchases, please contact Simon & Schuster Special Sales at 1-866-506-1949 or business@simonandschuster.com. • The Simon & Schuster Speakers Bureau can bring authors to your live event. For more information or to book an event, contact the Simon & Schuster Speakers Bureau at 1-866-248-3049 or visit our website at www.simonspeakers.com. • The text for these books are set in Cheltenham ITC. • The illustrations for these books are rendered in ink and watercolor. • Manufactured in the United States of America. • 10 9 8 7 6 5 4 3 2 • The Library of Congress has catalogued the hardcover editions as follows: • Barrett, Judith • Cloudy with a chance of meatballs. • Summary: Life is delicious in the town of Chewandswallow where it rains soup and juice, snows mashed potatoes, and blows storms of hamburgers—until the weather takes a turn for the worse. • ISBN 978-0-689-30647-1 (hc) • [1. Weather—Fiction. 2. Food—Fiction] I. Barrett, Ron. II. Title. • PZ7.B2752C [E] 78-2945 • Barrett, Judi. • Pickles to Pittsburgh: The Sequel to Cloudy with a Chance of Meatballs / by Judi Barrett; illustrated by Ron Barrett.—1st ed. • p.   cm. • Summary: Dozing off while contemplating Grandpa's unusual vacation, Kate dreams about Chewandswallow, where it snows popcorn and rains sandwiches, and the fate of the falling food intrigues her. • ISBN 978-0-689-80104-4 (hc) • [1. Food—Fiction. 2. Weather—Fiction. 2. Grandfathers—Fiction.] • I. Barrett, Ron, ill. II. Title. • PZ7.B2752Pi 1997 • [E]—dc20 95-40510 • ISBN 978-1-4424-0199-0 (bind up) • These titles were originally published individually by Atheneum Books for Young Readers.